THE ADVENTURES OF
KING ARTHUR

**Retold by
ANGELA WILKES**

**Illustrated by
PETER DENNIS**

Contents

2 The Sword in the Stone
8 The Lady of the Lake
14 The Knights of the Round Table
16 The Plot to kill Arthur
21 Sir Lancelot's Adventure
26 Lancelot and Guinevere
28 The Traitor Mordred
30 The Last Battle

Series editor: Heather Amery

The Sword in the Stone

Long, long ago, in Britain, when the world was still full of magic, there was a wise old wizard called Merlin. He could see into the future and work magic spells.

One wild and stormy winter's night Merlin was staying in a castle. It was the stronghold of his friend, King Uther. The Queen had just given birth to Uther's first and only son.

The King told Merlin he feared a plot to kill his son and that he had a plan to keep him safe.

Just before midnight, Merlin opened a small, secret door and slipped out of the castle.

Under his cloak he was carrying a bundle, and in the bundle was the baby boy.

The years passed and Uther died. No one knew he had a son to inherit his crown, so his knights fought each other to win the kingdom.

Far away in the Welsh hills, Merlin heard of these fights for the crown. As only he knew that Uther had a son, he set off at once for London.

There Merlin said to the archbishop, "The time has come to find the new king. You must call all the knights in the land to London."

The archbishop summoned all the knights to come on Christmas Day. Hundreds came and they crowded into the Abbey to pray. After the service, as they were leaving, they stopped in amazement.

A huge block of stone had appeared in the churchyard and in it was a sword. Round the stone were carved the words: WHOEVER PULLS THIS SWORD OUT OF THIS STONE IS THE TRUE BORN KING OF BRITAIN.

Eagerly the knights leapt on to the stone and one after another they struggled to pull out the sword. Even the strongest knights could not move it an inch. "The king is not here," said the archbishop.

"Send messengers round the kingdom," he ordered. "Tell every knight what is written on the stone. On New Year's Day we shall hold a tournament. Perhaps the king will be amongst those who come to joust."

3

Knights, with their squires, families and servants, rode to London from all over the land. They set up their tents on the field and practised for the tournament.

On New Year's Day the knights went to the Abbey churchyard. Each one tried to pull the sword out of the stone, but struggle as they might, no one could move it.

Among the knights who came to London for the tournament were Sir Ector and his two sons, Kay and Arthur. Kay had just been knighted but Arthur was only sixteen and was too young to be a knight.

On the way to the tournament Sir Kay suddenly found he had forgotten his sword. "I must have left it at the inn," he said. "I will fetch it for you," said Arthur and set off at a gallop for the town.

When he reached the inn, the door was locked. Arthur knocked but everyone had gone to the tournament. "I must find a sword," he thought. "This is Kay's first joust and he cannot fight without one."

He rode away, wondering what to do. Passing the Abbey churchyard, he saw the sword in the stone. Without reading the words on the stone, he leapt off his horse, ran to the stone and pulled out the sword.

Arthur galloped back to the tournament. "Here's a sword," he said, handing it to Kay. Kay stared at it for a moment, then looked at Arthur. He knew where the sword came from and snatched it.

He hurried to Sir Ector. "Look, father," he shouted. "Here is the sword from the stone. I must be the King of Britain." But Sir Ector knew his son well. "Let us go back to the churchyard," he said quietly.

In the Abbey, Sir Ector made his elder son swear on The Bible to tell the truth about the sword. Kay bowed his head and said, "Arthur gave it to me." Then Arthur told Sir Ector what he had done.

They went into the churchyard and Arthur put the sword back into the stone. Sir Ector seized it but it would not move. Then Kay tried but it still would not move. "It is your turn, Arthur," said Sir Ector.

Arthur gripped the sword, pulled and it slid easily out of the stone. Sir Ector and Kay knelt down at once. Arthur looked at them in surprise. "What is the matter? Why are you kneeling?" he asked.

"Read the words on the stone," said Sir Ector. "I am not your real father," he explained. "When you were a baby, Merlin brought you to me so that you would be safe from Uther's enemies."

"Now we must tell the Archbishop that we have found the King." But the other knights would not believe it. They went back to their homes, agreeing to meet again in London to settle the matter.

They met at Whitsun and crowds watched the knights try their luck. Only Arthur could pull out the sword. The crowds shouted, "Arthur is King!" And knights and people knelt to swear their loyalty.

The Lady of the Lake

So Arthur was crowned King and set up his court at Camelot. He gathered Merlin and all the best knights round him, and brought peace to the land. Anyone in trouble could go to his court for help.

One day a young man came to the court, leading a horse carrying a dead knight. The man told Arthur that his master had been killed by a knight in the forest who swore to kill every knight who passed.

"I seek revenge!" cried the man. "The knight, Sir Pellinore, challenged my good master, then fought and killed him. Is there any knight here who will punish him for my master's death?"

"Let me go," a young man called Grifflet begged the King. Arthur agreed and knighted him at once. Grifflet set off, but that night his horse came back to Camelot. Grifflet was badly wounded.

The next day Arthur rode into the forest. He was very angry that Grifflet had been so badly hurt. And he wanted to fight Sir Pellinore himself, in revenge for his knight's death.

Riding through the forest, he came to a clearing and saw three robbers attacking Merlin. Arthur charged at them and they ran into the trees. "Merlin, why didn't your magic powers save you?" asked Arthur.

"I did not use them," said Merlin. "But you are in far greater danger than I was. Sir Pellinore is one of the strongest knights in the world. Turn back." But Arthur rode on, so Merlin went with him.

Soon they saw Sir Pellinore's tent through the trees. Suddenly a mighty knight on a huge horse appeared in front of them. "I am Sir Pellinore!" he shouted. "If you come any further, I will kill you."

9

"We shall fight to the death," cried Arthur. He and Pellinore rode to opposite ends of a clearing, then they levelled their lances and thundered towards each other.

Each lance clashed so hard on the shields that they snapped. A squire brought new ones and they charged again. This time Arthur was thrown from his horse.

Arthur leapt to his feet. "How good are you with a sword?" he shouted. Pellinore jumped down from his horse and they fought on.

Arthur fought bravely but Pellinore was stronger. They hacked and slashed, then Pellinore gave Arthur's sword such a blow it broke.

"Now you are in my power," cried Pellinore. "Surrender or die." But Arthur rushed at him, threw him down and they wrestled on the ground.

Soon Pellinore had Arthur at his mercy again. He was about to cut off his head when Merlin cried, "Stop! You must not kill the King."

Pellinore looked at Merlin in surprise. "I must kill him," he said. "If he lives, he will never forgive me. My life and honour depend on it."

Merlin secretly cast a spell on Pellinore, who slumped to the ground. "A brave knight," said Merlin, "asleep he will do no harm."

Arthur lay on the grass, badly wounded. Merlin helped him on to his horse and led him through the forest to the home of a hermit. The old man dressed Arthur's wounds and gave him medicines to drink.

After a few days, Arthur was well enough to leave. "Merlin," he said, "what shall I do? I have no sword." Merlin smiled and said, "We shall go to the Lake of Avalon. There we shall find a sword for you."

Next morning, they set off and rode for many days until they came to a misty lake in the hills. On the bank, Arthur stopped his horse and stared in surprise. "Look, Merlin," he whispered.

Rising out of the lake was a hand, holding a magnificent, jewelled sword and scabbard.

Walking across the water towards them was a beautiful lady. "It is the Lady of the Lake," said Merlin quietly. "She lives in a magic castle under the water. You must ask her for the sword and scabbard."

They got off their horses, tied them to a tree and waited on the bank for the Lady.

When she came up to Arthur, he bowed and took her hand. "My Lady," he said, "I beg you to give me the sword." "It is called Excalibur," she said. "You may take it." She pointed to a boat hidden in the reeds.

Arthur stepped into the boat and, as if by magic, it floated across the water to the hand. Arthur grasped the sword and scabbard and at once the hand slid silently beneath the water and was gone.

When the boat brought Arthur back to the shore, the Lady had vanished. Joyfully he showed the sword and scabbard to Merlin. "Which do you like best?" asked Merlin. "The sword," said Arthur. Merlin frowned.

"You will win many battles with the sword," he said, "but the scabbard is worth more. While wearing it, you will not bleed, even badly wounded. Let us go," and they rode back to a great welcome at Camelot.

13

The Knights of the Round Table

The years passed and Arthur fell in love with the beautiful Lady Guinevere. "Merlin," he said one day, "I wish to marry Guinevere." "You will not always be happy together," Merlin warned him.

Arthur would not change his mind, so Merlin went to Guinevere's father, Sir Leo. "The King loves your beautiful daughter and wishes to marry her," he said. Sir Leo was delighted and gave his consent at once.

The marriage was to be at Easter and a few days before, Guinevere came to Camelot with many knights. Then she was married to Arthur and crowned Queen.

After the ceremony, Arthur led Guinevere to the great hall. A magnificent feast was laid out on a huge round table which Sir Leo had given Arthur as a wedding present.

Before the feast began, Arthur stood up and spoke to his knights. "From this great day you shall be known as the Knights of the Round Table," he said.

"Each knight must swear to be noble and brave, to fight for just causes and to always help the weak and those in distress. We shall meet once a year at Camelot to tell of our adventures and the Knights of the Round Table shall become famous throughout the land."

The Knights stood up and each one swore a solemn oath to follow these rules.

The Plot to kill Arthur

King Arthur had a wicked sister, Morgan le Fay, who was married to Lord Uriens. She hated Arthur and had fallen in love with a handsome knight, Sir Accolon.

Morgan decided to kill both Arthur and her husband, so that she could marry Accolon and rule Arthur's kingdom with him.

Accolon loved Morgan and would do anything she asked. He did not know she was wicked and knew evil spells.

One day Arthur and Accolon went hunting stags in the forest. By evening they were lost. Trying to find their way home, they came to a lake.

Floating by the shore was a strange, beautiful boat, lit by torches. Lovely maidens on the deck invited the tired men to eat and rest.

A splendid feast was spread out for them. They ate and then fell asleep, not knowing they were under the spell of Morgan le Fay.

When Arthur woke, he was chained in a dark prison with twenty knights. They told him they were the prisoners of a knight called Sir Damas.

Soon a maid came into the prison. "Sir Damas will set you free," she told them "if one of you will fight and kill an enemy knight for him."

16

"I will fight," cried Arthur. So the maid unlocked his chains and led him out of the prison. She gave him armour, a helmet and a sword. "Here is Excalibur," she said, "sent to you by your sister Morgan."

When Accolon woke, a dwarf offered him a sword. "Queen Morgan sends you this and begs you to fight an unknown knight for her," he said. Accolon took it and went to the battlefield where Arthur was waiting.

The two knights met with their visors down so they could not recognize each other. The battle began and Arthur fought fiercely but his sword was useless. Again and again he was wounded. Then his sword snapped.

Accolon raised his sword to kill Arthur. But, at that moment, the Lady of the Lake appeared, casting a spell on Accolon who dropped it. Arthur saw it was the real Excalibur, seized it and cried, "Now die!"

17

Arthur struck Accolon so hard, he fell down, blood gushing from his head. "Kill me, noble knight," said Accolon. "You have won." Arthur lowered his sword when he heard Accolon's voice and knelt at his side.

"Who are you?" he asked. "Accolon," the knight whispered. Arthur raised his visor and Accolon wept when he saw who it was. He told Arthur that he had been sent by Morgan to kill him and begged forgiveness.

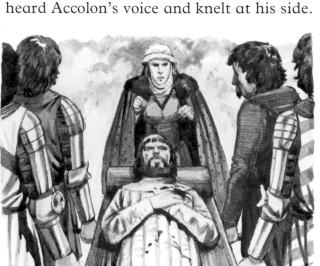

Then Accolon died from his wounds and Arthur swore revenge on Morgan. He sent Accolon's body to her. She was heartbroken when she saw Accolon and furious that Arthur had Excalibur again.

Determined to steal Excalibur, she rode to the abbey where Arthur was recovering from his wounds and asked to see him. "He is asleep," said a nun. "Do not wake him," said Morgan. "I will sit at his bedside."

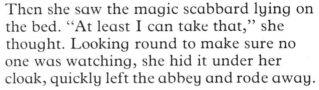

She crept quietly into the room where Arthur lay sleeping, hoping to steal the sword. But Arthur slept with it clasped in his hand and Morgan did not dare touch it in case he woke up and saw her.

Then she saw the magic scabbard lying on the bed. "At least I can take that," she thought. Looking round to make sure no one was watching, she hid it under her cloak, quickly left the abbey and rode away.

When Arthur woke up and found the scabbard gone, he called the nuns. He leapt up when he heard Morgan had been to the abbey. "Saddle my horse," he cried. "I will go after her. She must not escape."

Morgan soon heard Arthur and a knight galloping after her. "He shall not have the scabbard," she screamed and threw it into a lake. Then she used her magic to turn herself and her servant into huge rocks.

19

Arthur did not see the scabbard fall into the lake and rode past the rocks, searching everywhere for Morgan. He could not understand how she had vanished and angrily turned back towards Camelot.

That evening, a servant girl came to the court. "Queen Morgan sent me,' she said to Arthur. "She begs you to forgive her and offers you this jewelled cloak as a token of her love for you."

Arthur suspected it might be a trick. "You put it on first," he told the girl. "Oh no, Sir," she said, afraid. "Put it on," ordered Arthur. Slowly she did so and in a flash the cloak burst into flames.

Once again, Morgan le Fay's plot to kill King Arthur had failed. Angrily he banished her from Camelot for ever.

Sir Lancelot's Adventure

At King Arthur's court was a knight called Sir Lancelot. Strong, very brave and handsome, he won more tournaments, fought more battles and set out on more dangerous quests than any other knight.

Although he was King Arthur's most trusted knight, Sir Lancelot had fallen in love with Arthur's queen, Guinevere. Lancelot knew he could never marry her but had sworn to love and protect her always.

One morning Lancelot rode off in search of adventure with his cousin, Sir Lionel. By the afternoon, the knights were hot and tired in their armour. "Let's rest under this tree for a while," said Lancelot.

After tying up their horses, Lancelot lay on the cool grass and went to sleep. Lionel was leaning sleepily against the tree when he heard horses' hoofs. Then he saw a huge knight chasing three others across the plain.

The huge knight attacked the three other knights and soon defeated them. He tied them to their horses, then led the horses away.

Without waking Lancelot, Lionel leapt on to his horse and rode up to him. But the huge knight only laughed when Lionel challenged him.

Then he charged. Lionel fought hard but the knight was too strong. He tied up Lionel and led him away to a castle with the other captives.

Lancelot was still asleep and did not know what had happened. While he slept, four ladies rode by and stopped to look at him. "How handsome he is," they sighed. Each one wished he would fall in love with her.

One of the ladies was Morgan le Fay. "I have a plan," she said. "I will cast a spell on him so that we can take him, still asleep, to my castle. When he wakes, I will tell him to choose one of us as his love, or die."

When Lancelot woke from his enchanted sleep, he was in a dark dungeon. He did not know where he was or how he got there. He tried to find a way out but the door was locked and the windows barred. Then

the four ladies came in and ordered him to choose one of them as his love. "I can love no one but my Lady Guinevere," said Lancelot. Morgan le Fay threatened him with death but he would not give in.

Lancelot was left alone in his prison. That night the maid who brought his supper said, "Sir, I will help you escape if you will fight a battle for my father, who is a noble knight." Lancelot agreed at once.

Early next morning, the maid set Lancelot free and gave him armour and a horse. Then he fought the battle, winning easily. After saying goodbye to the maid and her father, he set off to look for Sir Lionel.

After many days, Lancelot met a maiden and told her of his search. "A wicked knight, Sir Tarquin, lives in a castle near here. He has captured many knights. Perhaps Sir Lionel is in his prison," she said.

She led Lancelot to the castle and, as they approached it, they saw Sir Tarquin, leading a captured Knight of the Round Table. Lancelot put on his helmet. "Defend yourself, Sir," he shouted.

Lancelot and Sir Tarquin charged each other so violently that their horses both fell under them. The two knights were thrown to the ground and they lay there for a while, stunned and unable to move.

Then they staggered to their feet and fought on with their swords. They struck blow after blow, wounding each other many times, but neither could win. After many hours they were too tired to fight.

"You are the bravest knight I have met," said Tarquin, "Let us fight no more." "Agreed," said Lancelot, "but first promise to free your captives." "I will if you tell me your name," said Tarquin.

When Lancelot told him, Tarquin cried out, "Then we fight on. Long ago I swore to kill you in revenge for the death of my brother." They fought on until Lancelot struck Tarquin so hard he died instantly.

Lancelot took Tarquin's keys and went to his castle. There he found Lionel and many other Knights of the Round Table locked in the dungeon. "You are free," he cried. "Come, let us all return to Camelot."

Lancelot and Guinevere

As the years passed, Arthur and his knights rode out on many quests, fought battles and won great victories. These conquests brought peace to the Kingdom.

Although they always fought bravely, some knights were killed or died of their wounds, and there were empty seats at the great Round Table.

New knights came to Camelot but some were not true to the oath they swore and plotted against their King.

The leader of these knights was Arthur's nephew, Mordred. He wanted to destroy the brotherhood of the Round Table and become king. So he plotted to cause trouble between Arthur and Lancelot.

Sir Lancelot still loved Guinevere but was loyal to his King. He knew that Mordred was spreading lies about him to make Arthur jealous, so he met Guinevere in secret. But Mordred's spies were watching.

Mordred went to Arthur. "Lancelot and Queen Guinevere are traitors to the king," he said. "The punishment is death. They must die." But Arthur would not believe him. "I must have proof," he said angrily.

That evening, Lancelot went to Guinevere's room. Suddenly there was a shout outside the door, "Arrest the traitors!" It was Mordred and his men. Seizing his sword, Lancelot fought his way out and escaped.

Mordred went at once to Arthur. "I have proof of their treachery," he said. Sadly, Arthur agreed to fight Lancelot. "But what about the Queen?" asked Mordred. "Traitors should die at the stake."

One grey morning, Guinevere was led out and tied to the stake. But just as the fire was lit, Lancelot and his men charged up. He cut Guinevere free and carried her away on his horse to his castle in Wales.

The Traitor Mordred

Although Arthur was secretly happy that Guinevere's life had been saved, he knew he must still fight Lancelot. Assembling his men, he set off for Wales but some knights sided with Lancelot against him.

There were many fierce battles but neither side won. Sad to see so many brave knights killed, Lancelot took Guinevere back to Arthur and then sailed to France.

The war should have ended then but Gawain, a Knight of the Round Table, hated Lancelot for accidentally killing his brother. Gawain persuaded Arthur to go to France to fight Lancelot there.

Before he sailed, Arthur sent for Mordred, and told him to rule the Kingdom until he came back again with his knights.

This was the chance Mordred had been waiting for. After a few weeks he spread the news that the King was dead. Mordred crowned himself King and said that he would marry Guinevere.

When Guinevere heard this, she fled to London and sent a messenger to Arthur, telling him of Mordred's treachery.

Arthur at once sailed back to England. When he reached the harbour at Dover, Mordred and his army were waiting for him. There was a terrible battle but Arthur won and Mordred retreated.

Gawain was badly wounded. Arthur knelt at his side. "I caused this trouble," Gawain said. "Forgive me and forgive Sir Lancelot. Your enemies would not dare fight you if he were here." Then he died.

29

The Last Battle

Arthur wept for Gawain; then marched off to fight Mordred again. When their armies met, there was a dreadful battle. At the end, only four men were still standing; Arthur, two of his knights and Mordred.

Arthur looked in despair at the dying and dead knights. Then, seeing Mordred still alive, he shouted, "Traitor!" and ran him through with a spear. As he died, Mordred struck Arthur a huge blow on his head.

The two knights saw Arthur fall and ran to him. Gently they carried him to a small chapel near a lake, where they could tend his wounds. Raising his head, Arthur looked round him and recognized the lake.

He handed his sword to Sir Bedivere, one of the knights. "Take Excalibur," he said, "and throw it into the lake. Then come back and tell me what you have seen." He lay back, knowing he had not long to live.

Bedivere took Excalibur down to the lake. Then he looked at it. "Why throw away such a beautiful sword?" he thought, so he hid it in the reeds. He went back and told Arthur he had seen nothing unusual.

"You have not done as I asked," said Arthur. "Go back". Bedivere returned, took Excalibur from the reeds and threw it far into the lake. As it fell, a hand rose out of the water, caught it and sank again.

Bedivere ran to tell Arthur what he had seen. "Now help me to the lake before I die," said Arthur. When they reached the shore a barge glided up. In it were four ladies. One was the Lady of the Lake.

Weeping, they laid Arthur in the barge. "Do not mourn me," Arthur said to Bedivere. "I am going to the magic Vale of Avalon to be healed." The barge floated away and Arthur was never seen again.

When Lancelot heard of Mordred's treachery, he sped back to England to fight for Arthur, but he was too late. Heartbroken, he went to see Guinevere. She too was heartbroken and gently refused his offer of protection. She had vowed to live in a convent. Lancelot went to live in a monastery. A few years later Guinevere died. Soon after hearing of her death, Lancelot died too.

Most of the Knights of the Round Table had been killed in battle. The few who still lived went off to fight in the Crusades. And they never met again at Camelot.

No one knew what became of Arthur after the barge carried him away. Some think he was buried at Glastonbury. Others claim that he sleeps in a magic cave in Wales, with the Knights of the Round Table sleeping round him.

Other people say Arthur was taken to the magic Vale of Avalon, where it is always Spring and where everyone is young again. They even say that Arthur still lives there, waiting until England needs him and his knights again.

© Usborne Publishing Ltd 1981
First published in 1981 by
Usborne Publishing Ltd
20 Garrick Street
London WC2 9BJ, England

The name Usborne and the device are
Trade Marks of Usborne Publishing Ltd.

Printed in Belgium